Contents

Other Books in
The Shoebox Kids Series

The Shoebox Kids

Adventure on Wild Horse Mountain

Written by
Eric Stoffle

Book 10
Created by
Jerry D. Thomas

Pacific Press® Publishing Association
Nampa, Idaho
Oshawa, Ontario, Canada

Edited by Glen Robinson
Designed by Dennis Ferree
Cover art and illustrations by Mark Ford

Stoffle, Eric D., 1963-
    Adventure on Wild Horse Mountain / written by Eric
Stoffle.
        p.   cm. —(The Shoebox Kids ; bk. 10)
    Summary: While on vacation at a ranch, the Shoebox
Kids investigate the mysterious disappearances of
DeeDee's dog Zack, meet an Indian girl, share their joy in
Jesus with the cowboy Shorty.
    ISBN 0-8163-1683-X (alk. paper)
    [1. Ranch life. 2. Dogs. 3. Indians of North America.
    4. Christian life. 5. Mystery and detective stories.] I.
    Title. II. Series.
PZ7.S8698Ad   1999
—dc21   98-43077
                                                    CIP
                                                     AC

99 00 01 01 03 • 5 4 3 2 1

Hi!

Wouldn't you like to go on a vacation to a horse ranch with the Shoebox Kids? But what if your dog ran away into the forest? Or was maybe dog-napped by a local Indian girl or her brother? And what if you were stuck on the mountain after dark—with a bear nearby?

In this Shoebox Kids book, that's what happens to DeeDee and the other Shoebox Kids. They learn about horses and about two kids who are different. When DeeDee's dog, Zack, disappears, she turns to Shorty, the tallest cowboy she's ever seen. While Shorty helps the Shoebox Kids learn to ride and handle horses, they help Shorty learn more about the kind of friend Jesus can be.

When an accidental meeting with a bear leaves them stranded on the mountain, the Shoebox Kids learn that even when you think you know someone, you can be surprised. And when you judge someone, you might be making a big mistake.

But can they find their way back down the mountain?

Adventure on Wild Horse Mountain is written by my friend, Eric Stoffle. His story will keep you guessing and help you learn some important lessons about judging other people.

Reading about DeeDee and the other Shoebox Kids is more than just fun—it's about learning what the Bible really means—at home, at school, or on the playground. If you're trying to be a friend of Jesus', then the Shoebox Kids books are just for you!

Jerry D. Thomas

1

A Vacation Adventure

"Come here, Zack! Jump in!" DeeDee called.

Zack was a year-and-a-half-old dog, but he still acted like a puppy. He jumped up and down excitedly as the Adamses loaded their sleeping bags and food into the car.

Finally it was time to go, and Zack was the only one left to get in. "Jump in, Zack!" DeeDee held out her hands.

Zack was so excited that he spun around in a circle before he jumped into the car and sat down on the seat beside DeeDee. DeeDee gave Zack a big hug.

"You don't want to stay behind," she said as she fastened her seat belt. "We're going to have too much fun. OK, Mom and Dad, we're ready. I wish we had a seat belt for Zack, too, so he can be safe."

"That is a very good idea," Mr. Adams said. "I'm glad you are being so conscious about safety. We'll have to find out if someone has invented seat belts for animals. For now, we'll just keep him riding quietly beside you. We can also ask Jesus to keep *all* of us safe on our vacation."

DeeDee and her mom and dad held hands while Mr. Adams prayed. "Dear Jesus, thank You for this vacation where we can spend time together as a family. We know You like fun times as much as we do, and we want to invite You to live in us this week. Please send Your angels to protect us as we travel."

DeeDee gave her dad's hand a tight squeeze. "Oh, and please take special care of Zack too."

"Thank you, Daddy," DeeDee said when she opened her eyes.

Mr. Adams smiled. "You're welcome, DeeDee."

DeeDee rode quietly in the car for an hour

and a half. She read a book from the school library about Indians and colored some pictures. Zack slept curled up in the seat beside her. She listened once in awhile to Mom and Dad as they talked about the exciting vacation they were going to have in the mountains.

DeeDee could hardly wait. It wasn't just her family who was going. The Vargases were going too. So were the Tans and Jenny and her mom and Willie Teller and his mom and dad.

"How much farther is it?" DeeDee blurted out.

Mr. Adams chuckled. "I thought you told us before we left that you weren't going to ask that question."

DeeDee put her hand over her mouth and giggled. "I'm sorry. It was an accident."

Mr. Adams slowed down and turned onto a winding gravel road. "Well," he said, "It looks like we are almost there. See that sign?"

DeeDee peered out the window at a sign that read *Wild Horse Mountain Retreat—12 Miles*. Zack woke up when he heard the gravel crunching underneath the tires and licked DeeDee on the cheek. "See, Zack," DeeDee said. "Only twelve more miles to go." DeeDee saw a cloud of dust ahead of them. "It looks like someone is just ahead of us," she said.

A few minutes later, they drove around a corner right behind the Vargases' station wagon.

"That's Maria and Chris's car," DeeDee shouted.

"It sure is," Mrs. Adams said.

DeeDee quickly packed her Indian book and coloring books into her backpack and petted Zack. "We're almost there, Zack. You're going to have so much fun too." Then she whispered into Zack's ear. "Don't you go running off and get lost in the mountains either, or I might never find you."

2

Wild Horse Mountain Retreat

Soon the Adamses pulled up behind the Vargas family in front of their cabins at Wild Horse Mountain Retreat. DeeDee saw that the Teller's van was already parked in front of one of the cabins. She hopped out of the car, and Zack followed right behind her. Zack ran over to greet Chris, Maria, and Willie. Willie had brought his dog, Coco, too. DeeDee grabbed Zack's leash and ran to catch up.

"Want to go explore after Sammy and Jenny get here and we are all moved in?" DeeDee asked.

"Sure!" Willie said. "I want to go find the horses. Dad says we can go for a ride tomorrow."

"Your dogs are so cute!" a strange voice said.

DeeDee, Willie, Chris, and Maria whirled around at the same time.

"Who are you?" DeeDee asked, her heart pounding twice as fast as normal. She hadn't realized someone was right behind them. The stranger was a girl with tan skin, jet-black hair, and beautiful, sparkling black eyes.

"My name is Ruth Thompson," the girl said, looking at DeeDee.

"I'm DeeDee Adams. This is Maria Vargas and her brother, Chris."

"And I'm Willie Teller." Willie introduced himself.

DeeDee tried to smile and act friendly, but she was still kind of upset. She was sure Ruth had meant to scare them by sneaking up behind them. Then she remembered the lesson at the Shoebox last weekend. *I guess I shouldn't be so quick to judge other people,* she suddenly thought. *Maybe Ruth didn't mean to scare us.*

No one said anything for a few minutes. Ruth acted nervous the way she shifted back and forth on her feet. She looked like a pine tree swaying in the wind.

"Anyway, I . . . uh, I just thought your dogs were really cute. I like dogs," Ruth said.

"Thank you," DeeDee replied.

Willie pointed at his dog. "That's Coco. He's really friendly. You can pet him if you want." Willie rolled forward and called Coco. "Come here, Coco. This is Ruth."

Coco stopped playing with Zack and jumped into Willie's lap.

Zack shook his head as if he was confused. Then he chased after Coco. But he skidded to a stop when Ruth knelt down in front of him.

"Who are you, little doggy?" Ruth asked as she reached out to pet Zack.

Zack wagged his tail and went right up to Ruth.

"That's Zack," DeeDee said. "He's *my* dog." DeeDee tried to keep from feeling jealous while Ruth petted Zack. Worst of all, Zack seemed to like Ruth almost better than he liked anyone else.

Suddenly, Ruth jumped to her feet. She stared off into the forest.

"What's the matter?" Chris asked.

"I just thought we were being spied on."

DeeDee shuddered. She noticed that her friends' faces looked worried too. "You mean there's something in the woods watching us?"

Ruth turned her head and smiled at DeeDee. "I don't think it's a ghost or anything, if that's what you're afraid of. I think it's probably just my brother. He likes to sneak around as quietly as he can in the woods."

"Why does he do that?" Willie wanted to know.

"Haven't you ever played cowboys and Indians?"

"Well, yeah," Willie replied.

"My little brother does too. Only, since we are really Paiute Indians, he likes to be the Indian. So he sneaks around in the woods. Sometimes he plays just by himself," Ruth explained.

"That sounds like fun," Chris said.

"My brother is pretty good at sneaking around. He's so quiet he can even sneak up on me before I know he's there. Sometimes he scares me so badly I want to catch him and wrestle him to the ground until he begs for forgiveness."

DeeDee couldn't help but grin. That's exactly how she felt when Ruth scared them. "I know that feeling," she said.

Willie was watching the woods to see if he could see Ruth's brother. But all he could see were trees, bushes, and wildflowers. He shrugged. "What's your brother's name?"

"Eagle Feather," Ruth said. "My mother is a full-blooded Paiute Indian. Our family gave us Indian names as well as more common Anglo names like you have. My full name is Ruth Running Deer Thompson, and my brother's name is David Eagle Feather Thompson."

"Is your family on vacation here?" DeeDee asked.

"We live here."

Willie's wide eyes looked around at all the mountains. "You mean you get to stay here all the time? Cool!"

Ruth shook her head sadly. "Not all the time. My mom lives here all year because she works at the lodge. But my brother and I go to California to live with our dad during the winter. That way we can spend time with both our parents and go to school too."

"I'm sorry," DeeDee said, when she realized that the reason Ruth lived in both places was because her parents were divorced.

Ruth sighed and changed the subject. "I heard you say you were going to find the horses. But the horses aren't at the corrals. A group of trail riders is due to get back today, but they aren't here yet."

"Are there any other fun places to see?" Willie asked.

Ruth pointed at a trail that curved around the cabins and disappeared somewhere in the forest. "That's a good trail to hike. It goes to a small meadow with lots of yellow and purple and blue wildflowers." Ruth glanced down at the ground. "Oh look, they're so cute!"

Coco and Zack wrestled in the dirt at Ruth's feet. Willie laughed. "It looks like Coco and Zack are having fun."

Ruth knelt down and petted Coco and Zack for a minute. Then she stood up and waved goodbye to everyone. "I better go see if my mom wants me for anything. Bye!"

Right after Ruth left, Sammy Tan and his grandparents arrived, followed by Jenny and her mom. DeeDee and Maria helped Jenny carry her sleeping bag and suitcase into a cabin while Chris, Sammy, and Willie helped Sammy and his grandparents unpack.

"Look at this," Sammy said after he had taken his suitcase and sleeping bag into his grandparents' cabin. He put a gray cowboy hat on his head. "What do you think?"

"You look just like a real cowboy," DeeDee said.

"Look at this, Sammy." Willie put on his own black cowboy hat. Sammy laughed.

When the Shoebox Kids gathered in front of the cabins, DeeDee said, "Is everyone ready to go exploring?"

"We sure are!"

Willie let Jenny hang onto Coco's leash, and they started up the trail.

"I love the mountains," DeeDee said. "I wish I could live up here all year long."

"I think you would freeze," Chris said. "During the winter, the snow probably gets so deep it covers the cabins."

"Then I wouldn't have to go to school," DeeDee replied.

Maria was following the trail behind DeeDee. "DeeDee, you would be *sooo* bored if you couldn't go to school. I know how much you like to learn."

"Maria's right," Sammy said. "You are the best student of all of us. You'd be bored if you couldn't go to school."

Suddenly Willie froze. "Did anyone hear that?"

"Hear what?" Jenny asked.

"I thought I heard a noise in the bushes," Willie said. "It came from right over there. And I thought I saw something move too!"

"I didn't hear anything," Chris said.

DeeDee shook her head. "I didn't see anything moving."

"Neither did I," Sammy agreed. "Stop trying to scare us."

Willie stared at the forest. "I'm not trying to scare anyone. If no one else heard anything or saw anything, then I guess I must be imagining it."

Unless it was Eagle Feather. Maybe he's watching us, and we just can't see him, DeeDee thought. She looked at Zack. But Zack didn't act like anyone was out there either.

Jenny looked at Coco, who was sniffing the air in the direction Willie had been pointing. "Maybe Coco smells something," she said.

"But Zack doesn't act like he heard or saw anything. And he doesn't act like he smells anything either. Zack is a good watchdog,"

DeeDee bragged. "If there is anything . . . or anyone out there, he would know it."

Willie lifted Coco into his lap and wheeled up the trail.

"OK, everyone, let's keep going," Chris said. "If you haven't noticed, it gets dark pretty fast in the mountains. Let's go a little farther and then turn around to go back so we don't miss supper."

"Chris is right," Sammy said, pushing his cowboy hat back on his head. "Let's go so we can get back for supper."

Ten minutes later, Chris stopped abruptly. DeeDee and Zack nearly crashed into him. DeeDee stopped as fast as she could, but Zack kept going and pulled the leash out of DeeDee's hand.

"What did you stop so quickly for, Chris?" DeeDee asked as she reached down to grab Zack's leash.

"I thought I heard something this time," Chris said. "But I guess it was just the wind blowing through the pine trees."

Just as DeeDee tried to grab Zack's leash, Zack raised his head sharply, his ears pointed ahead on the trail. In a flash, he bolted away.

"Zack! Zack! Come back here right now!" DeeDee called.

But Zack didn't stop. DeeDee and her friends could hear Zack barking all the way up the trail. Then, all at once, Zack stopped barking. The sudden silence was eerie.

Willie wrapped his arms around Coco in a bearhug so he wouldn't get away too.

Yip! Yip! Yip! Ruff, Ruff! Coco barked and tried to race after Zack, but Willie held on tight.

"What's the matter with you, Coco? Stop barking," Willie pleaded.

None of the Shoebox Kids knew what to do. They kept waiting for Zack to come trotting down the trail wagging his tail. But he never came back.

"I—I think something happened to Zack." DeeDee's voice quivered. "Let's go look for him."

DeeDee led the way, with Chris, Jenny, Maria, Willie, and Sammy right behind her. The sun dipped behind the mountains making it darker. *I'm not going back to the cabins until I find Zack,* she thought. *Even if I have to search the whole forest at night by myself!*

The trail wound slowly up the hill like a snake. Around every turn in the trail, DeeDee expected to see Zack waiting for her with his tail wagging. But after ten minutes, there still was no sign of Zack.

"At least the trail is wide and not too steep," Willie said.

"Zack wouldn't have gone too far," Jenny said hopefully.

Chris looked at the sky. "If we don't get back to the cabins pretty soon, our parents will be worried."

"Everyone *stop!*" Sammy whispered excitedly. He had been walking very slowly with his eyes glued to the trail looking for tracks.

The Shoebox Kids froze.

"What is it?" Willie whispered.

Sammy knelt down to inspect something on the trail. "Did you notice this, DeeDee?"

DeeDee bent down to look where Sammy was pointing. She shook her head. "I don't see anything."

"That's just it, DeeDee! Zack's tracks have vanished!"

3

The Disappearing Dog

"Zack couldn't have just vanished," DeeDee said, about to cry. She tried to act brave. Jenny knew how she felt, because her cat had disappeared once too. Jenny came over and put her arm around DeeDee.

"Don't worry, DeeDee. Zack will be all right. We'll find him."

"I know we'll find him," Chris said. "Let's ask Jesus to help keep Zack safe and help us find him again."

All the Shoebox Kids agreed, and they knelt down right there on the trail to pray.

After they had finished praying, DeeDee asked, "Do you think someone kidnapped Zack?"

"I don't see any other tracks," Sammy said. "If someone had kidnapped him, I think there would be some tracks or something."

"Sammy's right," Willie agreed as he held Coco tightly.

DeeDee wasn't about to give up. She also wasn't sure if she believed no one had kidnapped Zack like Willie and Sammy said. She knew they were just trying to make her feel better, but knowing Zack might have been kidnapped didn't make her feel better at all. She studied Zack's tracks again up to where they vanished. If Zack had gotten off the trail, he would have left tracks pointing in the direction he went. But the way Zack's tracks looked, it was as if he was running up the trail barking, and then he just disappeared. "How could he have just disappeared?" DeeDee wondered out loud.

"Let's go back to the cabins," Chris suggested. "Our parents are probably starting to worry. Plus, we better tell them what happened to Zack."

Willie turned his wheelchair around. Maria

glanced around one more time before she started back. Sammy stood up and followed Jenny. And Chris and DeeDee brought up the rear.

But before leaving, DeeDee knelt down and studied the trail again where Zack's tracks had disappeared. It was then that she noticed something very peculiar. Beside Zack's footprints was a small, smooth dent in the ground in the general shape of an hourglass. Only it was bigger on one end than on the other.

"That's odd," DeeDee said out loud, but no one was around to hear her. DeeDee slowly stood up. Then she ran after her friends to catch up. *What was the odd-looking mark on the ground?* she wondered.

By the time the Shoebox Kids got back to the cabins, it was so dark all they could see among the trees were dark shadows. Willie let Coco jump to the ground, and Coco ran circles around his wheelchair.

"I don't like the woods at night very much," Chris muttered, looking around him as he slowed down to a trot.

"Neither do I," Jenny agreed.

When the Shoebox Kids rounded the corner of the first cabin, they almost scared their parents to death.

"Where have you been?" Mrs. Adams asked worriedly. "We were ready to go search for all of you."

"Mom! Zack is lost!" DeeDee wailed. "He just disappeared!"

Mr. and Mrs. Adams stared at each other for a second. They looked confused. Mr. Adams narrowed his eyebrows as he looked at DeeDee. "What do you mean, 'Zack is lost'?"

"We were hiking up the trail when Zack jerked his leash out of my hand and ran away. We could hear him barking as he ran up the trail. Then he suddenly stopped barking. When we went to look for him, we couldn't find him *anywhere!*"

"We think he saw something in the forest, and that's why he took off barking," Willie added.

DeeDee nodded. "But when we looked for Zack, Sammy found where his footprints just disappeared. Zack wasn't anywhere around, and we couldn't tell which way he went."

Mr. Adams came up and put his arm around DeeDee. "It's all right, DeeDee. You don't have to worry about Zack because he is right here.

That's one reason we were so worried about you. When Zack showed up all alone, we thought something had happened to all of you. We were getting ready to launch a search party, and your mother wanted to call the police."

As if to prove he was all right, Zack ran over and tried to jump into DeeDee's arms.

"Oh, Zack!" DeeDee exclaimed. "You're all right! I thought you were kidnapped!"

"Kidnapped?" Mrs. Adams asked. "Where did you get the idea Zack had been kidnapped?"

"Well, we thought since Zack suddenly disappeared, someone might have kidnapped him," DeeDee tried to explain.

Mr. Adams frowned. "Are you sure you aren't all letting your imaginations run away with you? Zack came to our door a few minutes ago. He probably just chased a squirrel or some other small animal and lost you kids. So he came back here."

DeeDee knelt down and gave Zack a big hug. "I wonder," she whispered so only Zack could hear, "just what *did* happen to you."

4

Shorty the Cowboy

During breakfast, DeeDee puzzled over Zack's disappearance the night before. She knew Zack wouldn't have just run off. Besides, his tracks had just vanished right in the middle of the trail! And Zack was too smart not to be able to find them again if he had chased a squirrel or other small animal. DeeDee played with her cereal while she thought. She didn't even hear someone knocking on the cabin door.

"Hello, Chris. Hello, Maria," Mrs. Adams said. "DeeDee is just finishing her breakfast."

"Everyone else is finished eating and ready

to go ride horses," Maria said as she sat down at the table with DeeDee. "Do you want to go?"

"Oh yeah! I forgot about the horse ride!" DeeDee hurriedly ate the rest of her cereal. "Come on, Zack. Let's go!"

With his cowboy hat scrunched down on his head and his cowboy boots on, Sammy looked like a real cowboy. He already had his horse picked out. Its name was Thunder, and Sammy was brushing its shiny gray coat.

"There are four horses left," Willie told Chris, Maria, and DeeDee.

DeeDee climbed the corral fence to look at the horses. A pretty black-and-white pinto trotted around in circles. DeeDee glanced over at Chris and Maria, who were watching the horses too. She thought Chris was eyeing the pinto. *That's OK,* she thought, *Chris can have the pinto. I like the one with the white spots on its rump.*

Maria picked out a palomino mare that had come over to her when she called it.

"You decided who you want to ride?" A deep voice drawled behind them.

Startled, Chris jumped up to the next pole on the fence, and DeeDee accidentally let go and fell backward.

Two strong hands reached out and caught her. "Whoa, Miss," the camp wrangler said. "I didn't mean to startle you kids."

"I just . . . uh . . . didn't hear you walk up," DeeDee stuttered.

The wrangler's eyes twinkled as he laughed. He was tall with a red mustache and short red hair under his black cowboy hat. "My name is Shorty Wilson. I'm sorry I scared you."

Maria twisted around and hooked her arms over the top rail of the corral. "Your name is Shorty?" She couldn't believe it. Shorty Wilson looked like the tallest person she had ever seen! Even from where she was standing on the fence, she could see straight into his eyes.

Shorty nodded. "Yup!" He grinned. "Shore is. Everyone calls me Shorty. You kids call me Shorty too. None of this 'Mr. Wilson' stuff. I know it's proper and all, but it's no fun having a nickname like 'Shorty' if no one uses it."

After Chris, Maria, and DeeDee introduced themselves, Shorty grabbed three halters and lead ropes from the barn and entered the corral. He caught the black-and-white pinto first and handed the lead rope to Chris. "Tie Apache over there," he said, pointing to a hitching post beside Willie.

Next, Shorty caught Maria's palomino. "Tie Snowy next to Apache, Maria."

DeeDee watched her horse nuzzle Shorty when he captured her. Jumping down from the fence, she met them at the gate.

"Angel, this is DeeDee Adams. DeeDee, this is Angel." Shorty introduced them.

DeeDee ran her hand gently along the side of Angel's head down to the spot just above Angel's mouth that was the softest. "Oh, you're so soft, Angel," DeeDee said. Angel nuzzled her hand as if to agree.

"It looks like you two were meant to be pals," Shorty said.

Shorty gave DeeDee some treats to give to Angel. "Only feed her when she is being good," Shorty said. Then he gave DeeDee a brush and showed her how to properly groom Angel.

"Um, do you think Zack could ride on Angel with me?" DeeDee asked. "He'll be really good."

Shorty looked at Zack and smiled. "I think so. Angel won't mind as long as Zack doesn't mind."

DeeDee sighed. "Oh, thank you."

Shorty moved down the line of horses and Shoebox Kids to make sure everyone had done a good job of grooming their horses. Then he started with Jenny, showing her how to put the saddle blanket on her horse and then how to put the saddle on. None of the Shoebox Kids could put a saddle on without Shorty's help, though.

"Don't worry about being able to saddle your horses by yourselves the first time around," Shorty said. "It takes practice, especially when you're not even tall enough to see over the back of a horse," he added with a smile.

When the Shoebox Kids had their horses saddled and bridled, Shorty led his gray horse away from the other horses and showed them how to put their left foot in the stirrup and swing their right leg over the saddle. "There, that's how you climb aboard," he said before swinging back down to the ground.

"I can do that," Chris said confidently.

"All right, Chris," Shorty said, "you're next. Be sure and tighten the cinch first, though."

Chris tightened Apache's cinch like he had been shown. Then he led Apache into the open and reached for the saddle horn. He slid his left foot into the stirrup. "Watch this," he told everyone.

Chris pushed off with his right foot but didn't get very far. He tried as hard as he could to pull himself up and lift his leg over the saddle in one try but finally had to drop back to the ground.

Sammy laughed. "So that's how you get into the saddle, huh, Chris?"

Chris laughed too. "I guess it's more difficult than I thought."

A few minutes later, with Shorty's help, everyone was in the saddles. Shorty handed Zack to DeeDee and then climbed aboard his own horse.

Willie surprised everyone by being the best rider. He wasn't scared at all as he trotted Smokey around the corral. Before the trail ride, he reined Smokey to a stop beside his friends. "I think we should pray for Jesus to protect us while we're riding," he said.

DeeDee nodded. "I think that's a good idea."

The rest of the Shoebox Kids agreed.

"Do you want to have prayer with us, Mr. Wilson? I mean . . . uh . . . Shorty?" Jenny asked.

Shorty pulled up beside the Shoebox riders. "I've never prayed very much," he said solemnly. "I guess I never learned how."

"We pray all the time," Sammy told him. "It

felt funny at first, but now I think we would feel more funny if we didn't pray." He looked around at his friends. "Jesus is our special Friend. I don't know what we would do if we didn't know Him."

Shorty rubbed his jaw thoughtfully. "You know something, I think I see some logic in that."

"I'll pray," DeeDee said. "Everyone close your eyes. Dear Jesus, first of all, thank You for this great vacation in the mountains. Thank You that we could all come to Wild Horse Mountain together and have a fun time. Most of all, protect us while we're here and especially while we're riding horses. In Jesus' name, Amen."

"You talked just like you were talking to a friend, DeeDee," Shorty said with a puzzled look.

"I *was* talking to a friend," DeeDee replied. "Jesus is my best friend."

Shorty's forehead wrinkled up, and he looked very thoughtful. "Chris. Why don't you take the lead. Apache knows the trail to Fern Falls."

Chris laid the reins on Apache's neck to turn him just like Shorty had showed them all how to do. Then he gently nudged Apache in the sides with the heels of his boots.

Jenny got her horse, Magic, to walk behind Apache. Then Sammy fell in behind Jenny on the back of Thunder. Willie followed Sammy, and Maria made clicking noises with her tongue to get Snowy to start walking in line. DeeDee and Shorty brought up the tail end.

Shorty was quiet for several minutes. Then he said, "You know, DeeDee, I haven't prayed since I was a kid. The only time I ever heard people pray before is when they sounded as if they were talking to a god who shot bolts of lightning at people if they didn't do exactly what He wanted them to."

DeeDee twisted around in her saddle as far as she could to see Shorty. "In the Shoebox, we learn that Jesus loves us more than anything. That's why He died for us. Most of all, He wants to be our friend. Mrs. Shue—she's our teacher at the Shoebox—showed us that if we make Jesus our best friend, we will want to live like Him. That's easier than trying to be good because we're afraid of Him."

Shorty pushed his cowboy hat off his forehead. He squinted as if he were thinking hard. "DeeDee, I'll have to give what you said some thought."

The Shoebox Kids soon quieted down on the trail ride to Fern Falls. Up ahead, Jenny was twisting her head around to see all the pine trees and huckleberry bushes and wildflowers along the trail. Chipmunks scurried on top of fallen logs, watched the kids for a few seconds, and then disappeared into their hiding places.

"We're not going to hurt you," DeeDee said to the chipmunks. She scanned the tall mountains surrounding them and picked out the highest mountain. It stood majestically above all the other mountains as though it was the king. *That is Wild Horse Mountain,* she thought to herself. She patted Angel's neck. "Good Angel," she whispered. While she was looking around, her eye caught a movement in the trees. *Is Eagle Feather spying on us?* She stared harder, but there was no other movement. *Maybe it was just the wind,* she thought.

5

Danger at Fern Falls

Shorty Wilson helped the Shoebox Kids find trees to tie their horses to when they got to Fern Falls. Except for Willie. Willie got to keep riding Smokey.

"Wow! This is awesome!" Chris exclaimed when he saw the falls.

DeeDee peered down at the pool where the falling water splashed down. Water sprayed on the rocks, making them wet and shiny. "It looks like someone pouring a bucket of water into a sink," DeeDee said.

"Yeah, and it's splashing all over the kitchen!"

Maria added with a laugh.

"Look at all the moss growing on the rocks," Jenny said.

Chris pointed at the plants all around the bottom of the waterfall. "I can see why it's called Fern Falls," he said. "Look at all the ferns growing down there."

Willie urged Smokey as close as he dared to the bank and peered over at the pool of water. Huge pine trees shaded the waterfall. "Does the sun ever get down there?" he asked Shorty.

"Only for a few minutes a day," Shorty replied. "Ferns need cool, moist air to grow well."

Suddenly, Apache snorted and reared back. He bumped into Magic, and Magic whinnied loudly. Then Zack started barking at something in the trees.

"Hey, what's happening?" Chris shouted. He ran toward Apache with Shorty right beside him.

"Don't run right up behind Apache," Shorty warned. "You might frighten him worse if he doesn't see you."

Chris slowed down and started talking softly. "It's all right, Apache."

Apache tossed his head. He stared at Chris

with wild eyes, and then he started to calm down.

"He seems to trust you, Chris." Shorty looked pleased.

Chris smiled as he carefully reached for Apache's lead rope. "Good boy, Apache. Good boy. What scared you, anyway?"

The Shoebox Kids crowded around Shorty. "What happened?" Maria asked.

"Something must have startled him," Chris replied.

Shorty Wilson frowned. His red eyebrows narrowed, and he pushed his black hat back on his head. "I don't think Apache was just startled. I helped Chris tie Apache. There's no way he could have gotten loose by himself."

"Look!" DeeDee exclaimed. She pointed through the trees.

"I see something!" Willie echoed. "Let's go, Smokey!" Willie and Smokey charged up the trail like the Lone Ranger on his horse, Silver.

"Be careful!" Shorty called. But Willie wasn't listening. He rounded a corner and was gone.

Shorty didn't waste a motion. He jumped on his horse and galloped after Willie.

"I hope Willie doesn't get hurt," Jenny said.

"He'll be all right," DeeDee said confidently. "He's probably the best rider of all of us. I just hope he doesn't catch up to whoever scared Apache and Zack."

"Why not?" Sammy asked. He took his hat off and wiped an arm across his forehead.

"Because who knows what they would do to Willie." DeeDee looked really worried. "Remember what happened to Zack last night? I don't want Willie to disappear too."

"DeeDee's right," Chris agreed. "We'd better go see if we can help." He hurried and tightened Apache's cinch. Then he grabbed the reins and saddle horn to pull himself into the saddle. It only took him two tries this time. "I think I'm getting better at this," he said.

Maria untied Snowy. "If Chris is going, I am too."

"Me three," Sammy added.

Jenny and DeeDee untied their horses too. Suddenly DeeDee remembered Zack. "Zack!" she called. But he didn't come. "Zack's disappeared again!"

Jenny didn't believe DeeDee at first. But after she helped DeeDee search all over, she didn't have much choice. "What could have happened to him this time?"

DeeDee thought she knew the answer. She searched the ground where Apache had been tied and found what she was looking for. All of a sudden, it was very clear. "Whoever was out there wasn't after Apache," DeeDee said. "He was after Zack."

"But how did Apache get loose?" Chris asked.

"They untied him so we wouldn't notice Zack was gone until it was too late," DeeDee said.

6

Cowboys and Indians

With a look of disappointment written all over his face, Willie soon returned to his friends on the trail. Shorty was right beside him, and Zack rode on the saddle in front of Willie like he was a real cowboy too.

"Oh, thank you for finding Zack," DeeDee said. "I was so worried he was gone for good this time."

"We didn't catch the kidnapper," Willie grumbled. "But at least we did find Zack. He must have gotten scared by all the commotion."

"You weren't really hoping to catch the kidnapper, were you, Willie?" DeeDee asked. "I mean, it could have been dangerous."

Willie shrugged. "Smokey and I can handle anything," he said confidently, patting his horse on the shoulder.

"OK, Willie," Shorty said, laying a hand on Willie's shoulder. "I admit that you and Smokey make a good team. But it was still dangerous to take up the chase when you didn't know who or what you were chasing."

"But I do know who I was chasing," Willie argued. "I was chasing an Indian." He looked at DeeDee. "You saw him, too, didn't you?"

DeeDee nodded. "I saw someone in the bushes close to Apache. I thought maybe I saw a head with a feather sticking up. Maybe there *was* an Indian."

"It *is* always possible that Apache could have untied himself," Shorty admitted.

DeeDee shook her head. "You said that Apache couldn't have gotten loose without help. I don't think someone tried to kidnap Apache, but I think whoever it was untied Apache to distract us while he kidnapped Zack." DeeDee looked at Shorty. "Someone tried to kidnap Zack last night too."

"But an Indian?" Maria exclaimed. "Just because we're riding horses doesn't mean we have to play cowboys and Indians."

"Willie and I aren't imagining things, and we're not playing cowboys and Indians," DeeDee argued.

Shorty pointed down the trail. "OK. Let's not get into an argument. I think it's time we started back," he said. "And what's this about an attempted kidnapping last night?"

As the Shoebox Kids headed back toward Wild Horse Mountain Retreat, DeeDee explained how Zack had completely disappeared the night before.

"*Hmmm.* That sounds mysterious," Shorty said.

"But he was waiting for us back at the cabins," DeeDee added.

"*Hmmm.* Very strange."

DeeDee nodded. *It is strange,* she thought to herself. She studied Shorty's face for a long time. Shorty was Wild Horse Mountain's wrangler, but DeeDee didn't know how long he had been working there. *Does Shorty know who is trying to kidnap Zack?*

7

Setting a Trap

The next morning, DeeDee crept silently out of the cabin so she wouldn't wake her parents. Zack looked up at her with pleading eyes. "OK, you can come too," DeeDee whispered as she took the leash and hooked it securely on Zack's collar.

At the horse corrals, DeeDee climbed onto the fence and called softly. "Angel. Come here, Angel."

The appaloosa horse raised its head and stared at DeeDee. Then it nickered and walked over to her.

"Hi, Angel," DeeDee said, holding out her hand.

Angel let DeeDee pet her head and scratch her ears.

"Hi!"

DeeDee froze when she heard the strange voice behind her.

"Don't worry. It's just me, Eagle Feather."

DeeDee turned around and saw a boy her age with jet-black hair and black eyes who looked a lot like Ruth.

"I haven't seen you before," DeeDee said. "How do I know I shouldn't be afraid?"

The boy laughed and jumped up onto the fence too. "Because I wouldn't hurt a fly. That's why. I was with my mom yesterday. That's why I didn't come and say Hi to you and your friends. What's your name?"

"My name is DeeDee Adams. I live in Mill Valley." DeeDee narrowed her eyes like she had seen Shorty do the day before when he was puzzled about something. "Are you sure your name is Eagle Feather?"

"Uh-huh," Eagle Feather said.

"Are you Ruth's brother?"

Eagle Feather nodded his head. "You met my

sister, huh?"

"Yeah, she came over to meet us when we got here." DeeDee forced a smile. *Could Eagle Feather be the kidnapper?* she wondered. *Ruth said he likes to sneak around quietly.*

Zack tugged on the leash.

"Oh, I forgot to introduce Zack. He's my dog."

"Hi, Zack," Eagle Feather said. He waved at Zack. "I wish I had a dog."

"Do you have any pets?"

"No. My mom says we can't afford any, and Dad lives in an apartment building that doesn't allow animals."

DeeDee hopped down. "Here, Zack. Come and meet Eagle Feather."

Zack wagged his tail as Eagle Feather jumped down and knelt on the ground. Zack walked right over and put his front paws up on Eagle Feather's knee and got his ears and head scratched.

"Zack is usually scared of people he doesn't know," DeeDee said, surprised that he went right to Eagle Feather. "But he seems to like you really well."

Eagle Feather wrestled Zack to the ground, and Zack jumped back up, ready to play. Eagle

Feather picked up a stick and tossed it. Zack ran after it.

"What are those on your feet?" DeeDee asked.

Eagle Feather looked at his toes and then twisted his head to look at his heels. "What?"

"The shoes you are wearing."

"Oh! These are moccasins. They help me sneak around in the mountains because they're quieter than regular shoes."

DeeDee had an idea. "Can you sneak up close to animals?"

"Sure can." Eagle Feather looked proud. "I do it all the time."

DeeDee tried not to act too suspicious. "I should go back to my cabin," she said when Zack returned with the stick.

"Can I play with Zack?" Eagle Feather wanted to know.

DeeDee frowned. She didn't like it that Zack was so friendly with Eagle Feather. *What if Zack likes Eagle Feather better than me?* she wondered. Besides, she didn't want Zack to be out of her sight, especially after his repeated disappearances.

Eagle Feather noticed DeeDee's expression. "That's OK." He quickly added, "I have to go home and wash the breakfast dishes, anyway. It's my turn."

DeeDee knew she had made Eagle Feather feel bad, and she tried to make up for it by coming up with another idea. "I'm going back to my cabin," she said. "Do you want to come and meet my friends?"

Eagle Feather hunched his shoulders and shook his head. "Maybe later," he replied. Then he stuffed his hands in his pockets and shuffled down the trail toward Wild Horse Mountain Lodge.

"I feel really rotten," DeeDee said when she got back to the cabins. Chris and Maria were rummaging around in their van.

Chris poked his head out of the van. "Where did you go? And why do you feel rotten?"

DeeDee told them about meeting Eagle Feather and how she didn't want him to play with Zack. "Now I feel rotten because I don't think he has any friends," she said.

Maria hopped out of the van. "I found it!" She held up a Polaroid camera. "It was under the seat."

"Great!" Chris exclaimed. "I told you I grabbed it before we left home."

Maria looked at DeeDee. "Why don't you think he has any friends?"

DeeDee sat down on her cabin steps. "Well, I was thinking on the way back from the corrals that in a few days, we will all be going home. Probably all the kids who come here for vacation have to leave after a few days. He probably doesn't even want to try to make friends because they'll just go away."

"That's probably true," Chris agreed.

"May I see the camera, Maria?" DeeDee asked.

Maria handed DeeDee the camera. "Do you want to take a picture?"

DeeDee was concentrating hard. "I think I might have an idea how we can solve the mystery of who keeps trying to kidnap Zack."

Sammy appeared in his cowboy hat and cowboy boots. "Did I hear someone say 'mystery'?"

"Are we going to solve another mystery?" Willie echoed, rolling up in his wheelchair with Coco on his lap.

Maria waved for Jenny to hurry up and join them. "Come on, Jenny, we've got a mystery to solve."

The Shoebox Kids huddled closely around DeeDee as she explained her plan.

"I've got a question," Chris said when DeeDee was through. "What are we going to use for bait?"

Everyone looked at DeeDee.

Willie spoke up. "Or more precisely, *who* are we going to use for bait?"

8

Mysterious Snapshot

The next morning, the Shoebox Kids found Shorty cleaning out the horses' stalls.

"Can we go for another horseback ride today?" DeeDee asked.

Shorty rubbed his chin. "Well, I don't know," he drawled.

"Is there anyone else going today?" Willie asked. "If not, our parents said it was all right with them if you wanted to take us."

"No, I can't say as there is anyone else raring to go for a horseback ride today," Shorty said with a sly grin. "Let me see.... If you're all rarin' to go, what do you say to helping me get these stalls cleaned out? There are a couple of extra shovels leaning against the wall over there with the rest of the tools. And I've got an extra wheelbarrow out back."

"Great!" Chris said. He looked around at his friends.

Willie wrinkled his nose. "Speak for yourself," he mumbled under his breath.

"Phew." Jenny held her nose. She sounded like an elephant with a bad cold.

DeeDee stared at her friends. She couldn't believe they were making a big deal about cleaning up after a few horses. "Come on. You guys sound like a bunch of wimps. Haven't you ever had to clean up after your pets at home? I've had to clean up after Zack lots of times."

Maria rolled her eyes. "I think cleaning up after a horse is a little different than cleaning up after a little dog."

DeeDee looked at Zack and then at the horses. She started to laugh. "I guess there is a big difference."

"Uh-huh." Shorty cleared his throat. "I would like to bring up a very good point here that I want you all to consider."

DeeDee and the rest of the Shoebox Kids gathered around Shorty. Shorty was still rubbing his jaw.

"Many children beg their parents to get them a pet, like a cat or a dog or even a horse. Lots of kids who come up here want a horse for their very own." Shorty knelt down and petted Zack. "Now, I see that you love Zack very much, DeeDee, because you take very good care of him. But not all children, and even some adults, take good care of their pets. They let them go hungry, and they don't make sure they have their shots, or they might even take them to the pound to get rid of them."

The Shoebox Kids cringed when they heard how some animals were treated.

Shorty glanced at each one of them before continuing. "Pets require a lot of attention and love. But all that extra work is worth it because it keeps them happy. That's why I clean out the horses' stalls. Why do you take care of Zack, DeeDee?"

"Because I know it keeps him healthy and happy," DeeDee replied. "And I love him."

"Exactly."

Jenny walked toward the tools and picked

out a shovel. "I think I've changed my mind," she said.

"So have I," Willie agreed.

Soon all the Shoebox Kids were helping Shorty clean the horses' stalls while Apache, Magic, Angel, Smokey, Snowy, and Thunder stood around and watched.

After the stalls were cleaned, the Shoebox Kids caught and saddled their horses. DeeDee helped Jenny lift her saddle onto Magic's back, and then Jenny helped DeeDee saddle Angel. By the time DeeDee had put Angel's bridle on, everyone else was ready too.

Shorty was pleased. He walked around with a big smile on his face. "My, but you kids sure learned quickly how to saddle your horses. And by helping each other, you were able to saddle up without my help."

DeeDee untied Zack and led him to Jenny. "Will you lift Zack up to me after I get on Angel?"

"Sure," Jenny said.

Chris rode up beside DeeDee a few minutes later. He patted his saddlebags. "I've got the camera," he said. "I think we're all set."

"Good," DeeDee said. It looked like they were ready.

After the Shoebox Kids said a prayer for safety, Shorty led out. He took a different trail than the one that went to Fern Falls. DeeDee kept looking around to see if she could see anyone following.

Maybe the kidnapper won't show up after all, DeeDee thought.

Two hours later, Shorty turned off the trail. The Shoebox Kids turned their horses and followed him. Suddenly, the trees opened up before them.

"Wow! A lake!" Willie exclaimed when he saw the crystal blue water surrounded by tall pine trees.

"It's beautiful," Maria said as she stopped beside Willie.

Shorty smiled. "I'm glad you like it."

After everyone else had tied up their horses and gone to the lake, DeeDee pulled the camera out of Chris's saddlebags. Then she led Zack over to a shady spot under a bunch of pine trees and tied him up. Working fast, she placed the camera on a log and aimed it at Zack.

Suddenly, DeeDee heard a twig snap, and she ducked for cover behind the log. *It won't do any good if the kidnapper sees the trap I'm making,* she thought.

When DeeDee thought it was safe, she peeked over the edge of the log. All was clear. Hurriedly, she ran some string around the tree trunks so it was only an inch or so off the ground. Then she found a couple of pieces of wood and set them on each side of the camera so the string ran over the pieces of wood and over the top of the camera. She was almost finished. All she had left to do was lean a long stick of wood right over the camera button and rest it on top of the string. Now, when the kidnapper tried to kidnap Zack again, he would accidentally hit the string with his foot and break it. When the string broke, it would let the stick drop on top of the camera button and take a picture.

"There," DeeDee said to herself. "If anyone tries to kidnap Zack, I'll catch him on film." She smiled. It was the best trap she had ever made.

DeeDee didn't like the idea of using Zack to help spring her trap. But Zack was the only pet the kidnapper seemed interested in. She scratched Zack's ears. "Don't worry, Zack. I'll be right over there by the lake watching you." Zack licked her hand as if he understood. "You just let me know if anyone tries to kidnap you, OK?"

DeeDee whispered before she left.

DeeDee walked to the lake and sat down on a rock where she could see her friends and Zack at the same time. Zack sniffed the ground a couple of times and then lay down. DeeDee turned her head and watched Chris, Maria, Jenny, and Sammy see which one could skip stones the farthest. Willie sat on a log down by the lake with Shorty.

Suddenly, Zack started yipping. DeeDee jumped up. "The kidnapper! The kidnapper!" she yelled.

Shorty was so startled he jumped off the ground as if he'd seen a snake. "Where?" he asked.

DeeDee pointed at Zack and took off running. In five long strides, Shorty passed her as if she were standing still. Then a bright light flashed in the shade where Zack was tied.

"What was that?" Shorty yelled as he skidded to a stop, blinking his eyes.

"The kidnapper!" DeeDee replied when she caught up.

"No. I mean that flash of light! What was that?"

DeeDee was so excited she was out of breath.

"Oh . . . that . . . was . . . a . . . camera," she said between breaths.

"Now, what in the world is a camera doing out here in the middle of the forest?"

DeeDee reached down and picked up the Polaroid camera with the picture sticking out its front. "It was my trap to catch the kidnapper."

The rest of the Shoebox Kids caught up and gathered around DeeDee.

"Did your trap work, DeeDee?" Jenny asked. "Did you get a picture of the kidnapper?"

DeeDee's hands shook as she gently removed the picture from the camera. The little white rectangle was beginning to turn into a picture. "Here it comes!"

Chris and Sammy squinted. Willie had his arms around Chris's and Sammy's necks. He cocked his head to one side to get a better look, but it didn't seem to help. "All I can see is Shorty's stomach."

DeeDee's huge grin turned into a sour frown. "I was *sure* we would have a picture of the kidnapper!" she moaned.

"May I look at it?" Shorty asked.

DeeDee shrugged and handed over the photograph. "I guess. It doesn't show anything."

Shorty studied the photo for a long time before giving it back to DeeDee. "I'm sorry I got in the way."

"That's all right," DeeDee said. "I'm beginning to think trying to catch the kidnapper is a bad idea. The kidnapper just seems to be one step ahead of me all the time."

Shorty clapped his hands together and rubbed them. "Well, cowboys and cowgirls, it looks like it's time to start heading back. All of you be sure and tighten your horses' cinches before you climb aboard."

DeeDee put the camera in Chris's saddle-bags. Before tightening Angel's cinch, she went back to where she had set her trap and looked around. After a careful search, she saw what she was looking for. It was the same hourglass shape in the dirt, just like she saw on the ground the two times Zack had disappeared and at the corrals when she had talked to Eagle Feather. Now she thought she knew where they came from.

After DeeDee got on Angel, Chris picked Zack up and handed him to her. Zack sat proudly in front of DeeDee.

Maria rode her horse up beside DeeDee. When she saw Zack, she burst out laughing. "After riding around on Angel, Zack won't want to walk on his own four feet anymore."

DeeDee scratched behind Zack's left ear. "I think you're right," she agreed.

After the Shoebox Kids had saddled up, they got into a line behind Shorty and filed onto the trail heading back to the cabins.

"Hey, DeeDee," Sammy said.

DeeDee twisted around so she could look at Sammy, who was riding right behind her. "What?"

"Sorry your trap didn't work. It was a good idea, though."

"I sure wish it would have worked." DeeDee sighed. "Since I didn't catch the kidnapper this time, I'll have to keep a very close eye on Zack from now on."

But not catching the kidnapper wasn't the worst thing the Shoebox Kids had to worry about! A bear was eating huckleberries right around the corner!

9

Bear!

DeeDee had never *ever* seen a bear in the wild before. She had only seen bears in zoos behind cages. But there in the trail right in front of her was a black bear! DeeDee's eyes got as big as saucers.

"Shorty! It's a bear!" she yelled.

But Shorty's horse didn't like seeing bears up close any more than DeeDee did. Before anyone knew what was happening, Shorty's horse reared up on its hind legs, bucked a couple of times, and charged down the mountain.

"Whoa!" Shorty yelled.

But it was already too late. Shorty did a backward somersault off his horse and landed on his legs not too far from Angel and DeeDee. As soon as Shorty hit the ground, he yelled and toppled over on his side. The confused bear took one look at all the commotion and ran as fast as it could in the opposite direction.

DeeDee held tight onto Angel's reins and tried to speak calmly. "Wh—wh—whoa, Angel," DeeDee said. There was still a high squeak in her voice, but she thought she sounded pretty calm. Finally, Angel settled down. With Zack in one arm, DeeDee hopped down beside Shorty.

Chris and Sammy hopped out of their saddles, too, and crowded around. Shorty acted like he didn't want to get up.

DeeDee knelt down. "Are you all right, Shorty?"

Shorty shook his head. "I don't think so. I think my leg is broken."

All of a sudden DeeDee's heart began beating twice as fast as normal. "Are . . . are you . . . sure?" she stammered, trying to get the words out.

Shorty grimaced. "Yes, I'm sure, DeeDee. I don't think it's too bad of a break, but I can't walk, and I sure can't ride."

Even though she had her best friends with her, DeeDee still felt scared. *Now what do I do?* she wondered. And then she thought of something her dad had told her. "If something happens and you are scared, tell yourself to be calm. You can think much better if you are calm."

DeeDee told herself to be calm. She took a deep breath. *Wow! I feel better already. It really works!* Then she thought of something else her dad had told her to do if she ever got scared. "Dear Jesus, please help me know what to do. All of us need Your help right now."

DeeDee opened her eyes. Jenny and Sammy were looking at her. They smiled. They knew she had been praying.

"What do you want us to do?"

Shorty thought for a moment. "You know, there's a cave just a few yards away. It's not a very deep cave, but the mouth of it is wide. There is just enough of an overhang to stay out of the sun, and the rock walls will reflect the heat of a fire and keep us warm."

Chris was kneeling beside Shorty. "How do we move you, Mr. Wilson?"

"That's a good question," Shorty said. "First,

we better immobilize my leg."

"What does *immobilize* mean?" Jenny asked.

"It means to put a splint on my leg to keep it from moving," Shorty replied. "First, find a straight, sturdy stick. Then we'll tie it onto my leg."

Willie was still on Smokey. He backed Smokey up and began searching for a stick from horseback. The way he leaned over in the saddle and examined the ground, he looked like a scout from an old western movie.

"I found one!" Willie yelled. He pointed at the ground. "It's right here beside this fallen log."

Chris got the stick and laid it beside Shorty's leg. "What do we do now?" he asked.

"First, I need a way to tie the stick to my leg."

Chris frowned. "I don't have—"

"I've got it!" Sammy interrupted. "Chris, you and I can use our belts."

"That's a good idea, Sammy," Shorty said.

DeeDee and Chris did everything Shorty told them to do. Chris held the stick against Shorty's leg while DeeDee gently wrapped the belts around both Shorty's leg and the stick. It was hard to tighten the belts without hurting Shorty, though. Every time Shorty grunted because of the pain, DeeDee stopped.

"Go ahead, DeeDee," Shorty encouraged her. "You're doing a very good job. Maybe you should think about being a doctor someday."

DeeDee smiled. "Do you really think I could?"

"Sure do," Shorty replied.

While Chris and DeeDee finished putting the splint on Shorty's leg, Sammy, Jenny, and Maria led the horses over to the cave and tied them up. Then they gathered wood and built a fire to keep Shorty warm after it got dark.

While everyone else was busy, Willie thought he glimpsed Shorty's horse a little way down the trail, so he rode down to check it out. He returned leading Shorty's horse.

Once the splint was put on Shorty's leg, the Shoebox Kids gathered around and helped him stand up. Then they helped him keep his balance as he hopped and skipped over to the cave. DeeDee thought they looked about as coordinated as a bunch of clowns all trying to go in different directions.

At the cave, they gently helped Shorty lie on the ground. "Thank you," Shorty said. "I'm glad you are all here to help me. But now, it looks like you kids will have to go back to the resort for help."

"By ourselves?" DeeDee asked.

Shorty chuckled. "It certainly doesn't look like I'll be much help. I know you can do it. And if you run into Ruth Thompson or her brother Eagle Feather, they can help you find your way back too. If anyone can get you back to Wild Horse Mountain Lodge, Eagle Feather can. He probably knows this country better than anyone."

"But he's the kidnapper," DeeDee said before she could stop herself. She remembered the strange marks on the ground and knew they were made by Eagle Feather's moccasins.

Shorty chuckled, then coughed. "No, Eagle Feather isn't the kidnapper. For a while, I also thought Eagle Feather was guilty. But I couldn't prove it, so I didn't accuse him."

DeeDee frowned. "That's not what I did. I was sure he was guilty, even when I didn't have any proof."

"You thought he was a suspect, but you didn't have a right to say he was guilty unless you could prove it," Shorty said. He shifted his body to get more comfortable.

"When you and Willie said you saw an Indian in the bushes yesterday when Apache got scared, I finally realized that Eagle Feather was not the one who had been trying to kidnap Zack. He had gone with his mother to town the day before yesterday, since it was her day off."

Something clicked in DeeDee's head. "I remember. Eagle Feather mentioned that he was with his mother. He couldn't have been the kidnapper then. But I found his footprints everywhere the kidnapper was." *How many people wear moccasins around here?* she wondered.

Shorty frowned. "I have a confession. It was my fault your trap with the camera didn't work today."

It took a few seconds for what Shorty said to sink in. DeeDee narrowed her eyes at him. "What do you mean it was your fault? You mean you got in the way on purpose?"

Shorty nodded. "If your trap had worked, then Ruth Thompson and not her brother, Eagle Feather, would have been caught."

"But that's exactly what I was trying to do—catch the kidnapper," DeeDee huffed.

Shorty smiled. "That's true, I guess. You were hot on the trail. But I wanted to talk to Ruth before you caught her so I could tell her that I knew what she was up to. So when I saw you tie Zack to that tree instead of take him down to the lake, I figured you had probably set a trap for the kidnapper."

All this time I thought Eagle Feather was the kidnapper, DeeDee thought. *But why was Ruth trying to kidnap Zack?* Then something Shorty had just said made her stop and think. "What do you mean? Do you know why Ruth was trying to kidnap Zack?"

Shorty's blue eyes danced. He nodded. "Yes, I believe I do know why she did it. It's just an idea, though. Maybe through your investigation, you can find out what her motive was."

Chris had just brought in a load of wood for the fire. He looked from DeeDee to Shorty. "So you aren't going to tell us?"

"No."

DeeDee didn't know what to say. She had been so close to catching the kidnapper in the act. "You won't tell us?" she repeated.

"Sorry," Shorty said, shaking his head. "This is a mystery that is best left up to you to solve."

Once Shorty was made as comfortable as possible, DeeDee gathered the Shoebox Kids around. "I think some of us should stay here with Shorty until help arrives," she told them.

Chris nodded. "I'll stay here and keep Zack

with me."

"So will we," Jenny and Maria said.

DeeDee looked at Willie. "Do you want to go with me? I'm going to need someone along who knows how to handle horses."

Willie smiled. "Yup. Count me in, pardner!"

DeeDee laughed. "You sound just like a real cowboy."

"I'll go too," Sammy said, adjusting his cowboy hat.

DeeDee looked at the sky. "It's getting dark faster than I thought it would. We better get going."

"DeeDee, come here." Shorty was up on his elbow. "Remember that the horses have been over these trails many times. They know the way home, and that's where they'll go if you let them."

DeeDee knelt down beside Shorty. "I'll try to remember," she said.

"I'm telling you this because it can get so dark in these mountains that you can't see your hand in front of your face, much less the trail. You'll just have to trust the horses to get you home." Shorty's face got really white, like he was in a lot of pain. He sank back down on the ground.

DeeDee put her hand on Shorty's arm. "I'm going to trust in Jesus most of all to watch over us and you too."

"Thank you, DeeDee. Say, you kids wouldn't mind praying with an old wrangler before you go, would you?" Shorty asked.

The Shoebox Kids all smiled at once. Everyone knelt down where Shorty lay as DeeDee said the prayer. "Dear Jesus, we're all a little scared. Would You help us? Sammy, Willie, and I need to get help for Shorty. And most of all, Shorty's leg hurts a lot. Would you help him feel better? Thank You. In Jesus' name, Amen."

When everyone's eyes opened again, the Shoebox Kids could see a tear in Shorty's eye. They knew it wasn't because his leg hurt. They knew it was because Shorty wanted to know Jesus better.

Chris untied Angel and tightened the cinch for DeeDee. He held onto Angel's bridle while DeeDee mounted up.

"Thank you, Chris," DeeDee said.

Chris smiled at DeeDee to help her feel better. "You're welcome. You guys be careful, OK?"

"We will," Sammy, Willie, and DeeDee all

said together as they turned their horses toward the trail.

"Please watch Zack carefully for me, Chris, too," DeeDee added before she left.

"I will."

Willie took the lead on Smokey. He looked at the gray sky and remembered how fast it got dark in the mountains when the sun went down. He tried to find the moon, but there was no moon. Willie's stomach suddenly felt like it was tied in a big knot. "I hope we can still see the trail when it gets dark," he said.

DeeDee was riding second. "Maybe we'll get back before it gets too dark."

"I don't think we have enough time," Sammy said. "It took us almost two hours to ride as far as the cave. We only have about half an hour of light left."

Sammy's right, DeeDee thought. *We don't have enough time. If only Shorty's horse hadn't spooked, we would all be safe and sound with our families.*

DeeDee, Willie, and Sammy rode through the trees and brush without talking. The woods seemed to be getting strangely quiet. DeeDee hoped it was so quiet because the birds were tired out from singing all day and all the other animals were tired from playing and had gone to bed.

She watched Angel's ears. Her right ear went forward; then her left ear went backward. Angel's hearing was so good she could hear things in the mountains DeeDee couldn't hear at all. But Angel didn't seem to be concerned. *If Angel isn't worried,* she thought, *then I guess I shouldn't be so worried either.*

Suddenly Sammy's horse kicked a rock that went bouncing off into the bushes. DeeDee jerked straight up. She had gotten so used to rocking in the saddle as Angel plodded along that the rock startled her.

"It was just a rock," Sammy said.

"I thought it was another bear or something." DeeDee twisted around to look at Sammy. It was so dark she could barely see Sammy even though he was riding only ten feet away. "Are you OK?"

Sammy nodded. "Yeah. I sure wish we were back at the cabins, though."

"So do I," DeeDee said.

10

Meeting the Kidnapper

"*DeeDee! Hey, DeeDee! Stop!*"

DeeDee stopped Angel and whipped around in the saddle. "What?"

"What do you mean 'what'?" Sammy asked. "I didn't say anything."

"Didn't you or Willie call my name?"

"No," Sammy said.

"I didn't either," Willie said. "But I heard someone."

"DeeDee, it's me." Ruth Thompson stepped out from behind a tree. She looked uneasy, like she wanted to run away.

The first thing DeeDee thought of doing was to tell Ruth off for trying to kidnap Zack, but she decided not to. She decided she shouldn't be so quick to judge people anymore. "Hi, Ruth. What are you doing here?"

Ruth shrugged. "I guess I wanted to say that I'm sorry for trying to kidnap Zack. Will you forgive me?"

DeeDee didn't mean to take so long answering, but she wasn't sure at first if she wanted to forgive Ruth or not. Then she thought about how she had been accusing Eagle Feather when he wasn't even guilty. She knew she owed him an apology too. "Yes, I forgive you."

Ruth smiled. It was the first time DeeDee had ever seen her smile. "Thank you, DeeDee," Ruth said. Then she looked at Willie and Sammy and DeeDee. "How come there are just three of you? And what took you so long? I've been waiting here for a couple of hours."

"A bear scared Shorty's horse," Sammy said.

"Then Shorty fell off and broke his leg," Willie added.

"And now we're trying to find our way back to the lodge to get help," DeeDee finished. "Will you help us?"

"Sure," Ruth said. "Can I ride behind you on Angel?"

DeeDee took her foot out of the stirrup and held out her hand for Ruth. Ruth grabbed DeeDee's hand and stuck her foot in the stirrup as DeeDee helped her up. DeeDee noticed Ruth's foot and started laughing. "You're wearing moccasins too!"

Ruth's face turned red. "Yeah. I guess you found my tracks, huh?"

DeeDee nodded. "Uh-huh. Do you think Eagle Feather will forgive me for accusing him of being the kidnapper? I was sure it was his tracks I had found everywhere."

"I'm sure he will," Ruth said. "It sounds to me like we all made some mistakes and need to be forgiven."

"That's for sure," DeeDee agreed. "Are you ready to ride?"

"I'm ready! Let's ride!" Ruth said.

Pretty soon, it was so dark DeeDee couldn't see Willie or Sammy at all, even though she could still hear their horses. She was glad Ruth was riding with her. It made her feel better knowing that Ruth knew where they were.

Once, Willie stopped because he thought

Smokey had lost the trail.

"I think we need to go left," Willie decided. "But Smokey wants to go right."

"We better go the way Smokey wants to go," Ruth said.

Willie sighed. "OK." He turned to the right.

Fifteen minutes later, they saw lights ahead of them.

"We made it!" DeeDee shouted. "We made it, Willie and Sammy!"

"I'll go tell our parents what happened and that we're all safe," Willie said as he turned Smokey toward the cabins.

"Good idea," DeeDee said. "We'll go get help for Shorty."

DeeDee, Ruth, and Sammy rode down to the lodge. DeeDee let Ruth down. Then she and Sammy got down and followed Ruth inside.

The first person to see them was a big man with a beard and a red flannel shirt. "Hey, are you the kids everyone's so worried about? The ones who went on a ride with Shorty Wilson?"

DeeDee gulped. "Uh . . . yes, sir. Shorty's got a broken leg. He's in a cave by the trail that goes to the lake. Some of our friends stayed with him."

The big man jumped to his feet. His voice boomed in the lodge. "I need some volunteers. Sounds like Shorty could use some help tonight." Before leaving, he turned and smiled down at DeeDee. "Don't worry, we'll take over from here. It was mighty brave of you kids to ride out of the mountains at night like that."

DeeDee smiled. "Thank you, sir."

"Thank you," Sammy said.

Back at the Shoebox

"Anyway, that's part of what happened when we got back," DeeDee explained to Mrs. Shue the next weekend at church.

"Is that all?" Mrs. Shue asked.

DeeDee lowered her eyes. "No. I guess I learned a lesson too. Ruth wanted to explain why she was trying to kidnap Zack. So she took me to meet her mom the next morning. I guess I didn't realize that there are lots of people who have a lot less than I do. And sometimes it's just too expensive to have a pet."

"It takes a lot of time and money to care for

a pet. Lots of people forget about food and veterinary bills," Mrs. Shue added.

"That's right," DeeDee agreed. "Anyway, since Ruth and Eagle Feather's mom couldn't afford to keep a pet, Ruth decided she would kidnap one for her brother to play with. She thought she could keep Zack in a secret hiding place."

DeeDee paused and took a deep breath. "The lesson I learned was that I shouldn't judge people."

Sammy cleared his throat. "That's a good lesson for us all to learn."

Jenny, Chris, Willie, and Maria agreed.

"On our last night there, we invited Ruth and her brother and her mother over for supper with us," Sammy said.

"And Shorty too," Jenny added.

"I tried to show him how to drive a wheel-chair." Willie tried not to laugh. "But I think I'm better at riding horses than he is at driving wheelchairs. He kept running into stuff."

"That's very true." A deep voice drawled behind the Shoebox Kids.

Everyone laughed as the tall man with a red mustache and red hair furrowed his bushy red eyebrows thoughtfully. "Thank you for inviting me to church," Shorty said. "You kids have really helped me to believe in Jesus again."

DeeDee wondered if she saw a tear in Shorty's eye.

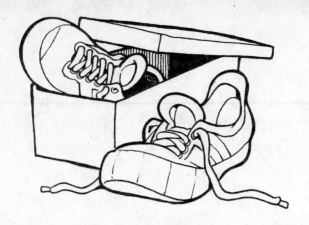

Whoever said the Bible was boring didn't know about The Shoebox Kids

Inspired by the series of stories in Primary Treasure by Jerry D. Thomas, The Shoebox Kids book series have been helping children like yours understand the lessons of the Bible for years.

Following the adventures of Chris, Maria, DeeDee, Willie, Jenny, and Sammy in these books is more than just fun—it leads to new discoveries about what the Bible really means at home, at school, or on the playground.

If your child wants to be a friend of Jesus, The Shoebox Kids books are just for you.

Get each one.
Paperback. US$6.99, Can$9.99 each.
Available at your local ABC. Call 1-800-765-6955 to order.

Book 1 - ***The Case of the Secret Code***
  Topic: Prayer. 0-8163-1249-4
Book 2 - ***The Mysterious Treasure Map***
  Topic: Baptism. 0-8163-1256-7
Book 3 - ***Jenny's Cat-napped Cat***
  Topic: Forgiveness. 0-8163-1277-X
Book 4 - ***The Missing Combination Mystery***
  Topic: Jealousy. 0-8163-1276-1
Book 5 - ***The Broken Dozen Mystery***
  Topic: Helping others. 0-8163-1332-6
Book 6 - ***The Wedding Dress Disaster***
  Topic: Commitment. 0-8163-1355-5
Book 7 - ***The Clue in the Secret Passage***
  Topic: Bible. 0-8163-1386-5
Book 8 - ***The Rockslide Rescue***
  Topic: Trust in God. 0-8163-1387-3
Book 9 - ***The Secret of the Hidden Room***
  Topic: Prejudice. 0-8163-1682-1
Book 10 - ***Adventure on Wild Horse Mountain***
  Topic: Judging Others. 0-8163-1683-X

Animal Stories
the Whole Family Can Enjoy!

It all started with a perfectly pesky pet parrot named Julius, and his pal Mitch. Then came a rascally red fox, a wildly wacky raccoon, a curiously comical cow, and a thunder cat by the name of Thor! But all of them help kids celebrate God's creation with laughter and wonder. Collect the entire "herd' and get a belly laugh or two yourself from the **Julius & Friends** series.

Paperback. US$6.99, Can$9.99 each.

Book 1 - *Julius, the Perfectly Pesky Pet Parrot*. 0-8163-1173-0
Book 2 - *Julius Again!* 0-8163-1239-7
Book 3 - *Tina, the Really Rascally Red Fox*. 0-8163-1321-0
Book 4 - *Skeeter, the Wildly Wacky Raccoon*. 0-8163-1388-1
Book 5 - *Lucy, the Curiously Comical Cow*. 0-8163-1582-5
Book 6 - *Thor, the Thunder Cat*. 0-8163-1703-8

Available at your local ABC. Call 1-800-765-6955 to order.